CU00252908

Reggie Rub
the Pirate of the Trees

Lucia Wilson

Illustrated by Frans Wesselman

Maymyo Publications

ISBN: 9798842466238

Publisher: Maymyo Publications

Author: Lucia Wilson

Illustrator: Frans Wesselman

Reggie Ruby, the Pirate of the Trees was written with the kind support of Mr Saurabh Jain, consultant ophthalmologist, who advised on the factual elements related to strabismus (also known as squint). www.saurabhjain.co.uk

This book is dedicated to trees. They take care of us and give us joy. We need to love and protect them.

It is also dedicated to all those who work so hard to support patients with strabismus and other eye conditions.

CHAPTER ONE

Reggie da Silva loves trees.

He shares his love of trees with his father, Laurence, who often talks to Reggie about the trees in his hometown of Dishergarh, West Bengal. Dishergarh is a tiny place in India, too small to find on a map of the world but more than big enough to fill Laurence's heart with wonderful memories.

"Plane trees, banyans, chir pine, neem, sundari trees," Laurence would almost sing the names as he gently taps out a rhythm because it makes him so happy, so Reggie would sing them, too.

These days, Laurence lives with his family in London and it's very different to Dishergarh. However, it also has many wonderful trees, and, as the senior park keeper in one of the biggest parks in London, Laurence is a happy man.

"Oak trees, yew, horse chestnut, silver birch, weeping willow trees" Laurence would sing, to a different tune, and Reggie would sing the names, as well, echoing his father.

Reggie's favourite tree is the one outside his bedroom window, a giant oak. Corrine, Laurence's wife, often teases him and says he only chose the house because of the oak tree! Laurence always laughs when she says this because he knows it's true. Reggie also loves this tree because of the wonderful tree house that his father made for him, but they call it a *boat-treehouse* because it's shaped like a ship.

"A perfect ship for Reggie Ruby, the pirate of the trees!" said Laurence, when he showed it to Reggie for the first time. And from that day on, Reggie's pet name was Reggie Ruby.

CHAPTER TWO

One morning, Reggie noticed something strange. He was standing in the garden and looking back at the oak tree but, instead of seeing one tree, he saw two! It frightened him, so he decided not to tell anyone. As time went on, Reggie became clumsier, which made him feel embarrassed. This made him grow quieter and he often hid his face with his hair and kept his head bowed low.

Corrine and Laurence became worried because when they asked Reggie what was wrong, he wouldn't say. So, one evening, Reggie's Dad decided to climb the tree, dressed as a pirate to see if he could work out what was troubling his son. He called out to Reggie from the boat-treehouse.

"Ahah, I be Captain Diamond, I'm looking for a pirate called Reggie Ruby, do you know where 'e be?"

Reggie managed a half-smile but kept his head low.

"Oh, Dad, I know it's you, don't be silly."

"Silly? Me? You come over 'ere and say that, Reggie Ruby!" said Laurence, stretching out his hand.

Reggie finally gave in and reached for his father's hand (which looked like two hands for some reason, just like the tree did sometimes) and he started to fall towards the ground! Laurence was horrified and covered his eyes with the shock, so he didn't see the wonderful thing that happened next; the giant oak tree stretched out its lower branches to catch Reggie as he fell. Then, ever so gently, the mighty oak placed Reggie on the ground and whispered to Reggie,

"Don't tell your father."

Laurence uncovered his eyes slowly and was astonished to see Reggie safe and unharmed on the ground. He scrambled out of the boat-treehouse and grabbed Reggie, then anxiously checked him all over.

"Are you okay, Reggie? Does it hurt anywhere?"

"No, Dad, I'm fine."

"But, but… I don't understand! What happened?"

At that moment, Reggie's mum came out to the garden and looked puzzled.

"Reggie! Why aren't you in bed? Honestly, Laurence, this is not the time for playing pirate games!"

Laurence scratched his head and scooped up Reggie to take him back to his bed, and as they all walked back to the house, Reggie looked at the oak tree and saw the lower branches give him a small wave. He waved back, without saying a word.

CHAPTER THREE

The next morning after breakfast, Reggie was about to look for his school bag when his mum stopped him.

"You're not going to school today, Reggie, we're taking you to see a nice doctor."

"A doctor?" said Reggie, "But why?" He wasn't a fan of doctors, they tended to do a lot of prodding, and looking in your ears and stuff.

"Your Dad and I think you need to have your eyes checked."

"Yes, Reggie," said his dad who arrived in the kitchen, fastening his tie.

Reggie thought this was a bad sign as his dad never wore a tie normally, usually he wore jeans and clothes that were good for climbing trees.

"I think you might have something wrong with your eyes. I don't understand why you missed my hand when you fell yesterday."

And, under his breath to his wife, he said,

"And I still don't understand how he wasn't badly hurt when he landed, I couldn't bear to watch."

At the hospital, Reggie waited with his parents for the appointment with the 'eye doctor' who had another name, something like "optalologist," or "ophthaloloogist" ; Reggie thought it sounded funny and made-up. While they waited, Reggie went to play with the toys in the waiting area. There was a girl his age who was also waiting to see the "optomalologist." Reggie noticed that, just like him, Alice seemed to be hiding her face, keeping her head bowed.

"Hello, I'm Reggie."

"Oh, hello, my name's Alice."

Alice looked up and Reggie noticed something unusual about her eyes; one of her eyes seemed to be looking in a different direction to the other one. Alice caught him staring and she dropped the toy in her hand and was about to go back to her parents, but Reggie spoke quickly, in a very gentle voice,

"Alice, can you see double like me? Is that why you are seeing this optoologalist?"

Alice smiled and shook her head. Alice was about to speak again but a nurse called out,

"Reggie da Silva, please."

Reggie just had time to wave goodbye to Alice and then they all went in to meet a man called Mr June.

"I thought he was a doctor," whispered Reggie to his dad, "why's he not called Doctor June then, why's he only a Mister?
"Shush, Reggie" he whispered back.

"Hello, hello," said Mr June, who was really jolly and kind.

Let's have a look at you, Reggie," and he started doing all sorts of interesting tests with strange machines that made Reggie look like a robot. He was fascinated because after trees, he really loves machines. Next Mr June moved his fingers around like a hypnotist and Reggie soon forgot to keep his head low.

"Okay," said Mr June turning to Corrine and Laurence, "Reggie has a squint. We also call it strabismus. It can, occasionally, cause double vision in some children. That would explain a lot."

"So, what does that mean, what can Reggie see?" asked Laurence, with a worried expression.

"Well, you told me he had an accident, yes? He missed your hand when you reached out to him, yes? That will be because he saw two overlapping images of your hand and reached for what we might call the 'ghost' image. I think he will have had this for some time."

"And can you fix it, Mr June?"

"Oh, yes, don't worry. We can fix it. Sometimes these things are corrected by themselves.

However, I would like Reggie to have some glasses for the time being. I'll ask one of my colleagues to help you with this if you'll just take a seat in the waiting room. We'll also book a follow-up appointment so we can see how Reggie is doing," said Mr June with a smile.

"Ok, thank you, Mr June, that is so reassuring," said Corrine, as Laurence shook his hand.

"What did he say? What does it mean?" asked Reggie as they left the room.

"Nothing to worry about, Reggie Ruby! Ahaaah!" and Laurence swept Reggie off the ground and gave him a big hug.

CHAPTER FOUR

The next day, Reggie woke up to the sound of tapping. He thought it was his Mum trying to wake him up for school, but then he remembered it was Saturday and still early. He threw the bed clothes off and realised the tapping was coming from the window! It was the oak tree.

Excitedly, Reggie rushed to the window and opened it.

"Good morning, Reggie!" said the tree with a low, rustling whisper.

"Good morning," whispered Reggie in return. "Oh, and thank you so much for saving me from falling the other day!"

"You're welcome, Reggie. Now, perhaps you can help me with something" and stretched out a branch for Reggie to grasp. "Oh, and be careful...with your double vision, I mean."

"How do you know about that?" Said Reggie in a surprised voice.

"Wasn't I a witness when you fell?" said the tree in a matter-of-fact tone.

"That's true. I'll see better when I get my glasses. Mum and Dad ordered a really cool pair yesterday," said Reggie as he stepped into the branches and found himself in front of a small door in the trunk of the tree.

"I've never noticed this door before," said a puzzled Reggie.

"That's because I only make it visible to special guests. Go ahead, Reggie."

When Reggie opened the door, he stepped into a large room with a small table. He saw four children and one of them was Alice from the hospital!

"Hello, Reggie, we've been waiting for you."

"Blimey, Alice, this is very confusing! What do you mean you've been waiting for me?"

"Come and have some breakfast and then I'll tell you."

Reggie was very hungry and helped himself to toast, jam, and apple juice while Alice explained the situation.

"Reggie, your oak tree is known as the Tree King, and he has been looking for five children with special qualities. Each one of us had to find one other child to join our team. I nominated you."

"Oh, why, was it because we both have strab moths?

"Ha ha… you mean strabismus. No, not because of that. I chose you because you are kind, and you love trees."

"Now, Reggie," said the Tree King, "let me explain what I need you to do. Our urban forest is in danger and my kingdom is under threat if we do not act quickly. Take a look at that screen over there."

Reggie looked at a screen which showed some shadowy figures at night, a tall man, and a group of animals.

"What animals are they? They look a bit like beavers," said Reggie.

"They are beavers, well-spotted" said one of the other boys. "I'm Henry, from Nigeria. Everyone calls me Egg."

"It's because he's so clever! He's a real egghead. And I'm Stella from Bologna, ciao, Reggie," said the other girl, "from the Italian branch!" she added with a chuckle.

"Philip," said the third boy, extending his hand to Reggie.

"So," resumed Egg, "now that you know everyone, let me explain our mission."

Reggie felt a shiver run all the way down his spine when he heard the word 'mission.' It made him feel like a superhero!

"We must save the urban forest. The urban forest, just to be clear, means the trees that grow in our city. Some are in parks; some are in streets and other public areas. Right now, there is one person in London who has been destroying trees in secret, usually at night, and he's been hiring the Rogue Beavers who can destroy a tree in a matter of minutes."

Egg pointed towards the unclear figure on the screen.

"This is Lewis Nero. Lewis Nero absolutely *hates* trees.

He has already destroyed more than twenty trees this year... sorry, your Majesty, perhaps you prefer to speak?"

"No, carry on, Egg, you're doing very well," said the Tree King.

Thank you, Sir. Nero is an architect, but no one will let him build any more buildings because his ideas are so destructive. He was working on a project in a leafy street, and he tried to have all the trees cut down because he said they were too untidy!

Fortunately, he was stopped by the local council who refused him permission to chop down the trees, but now he's gone completely mad and he's cutting down trees all over London."

"And we can't let him destroy any more," said Alice.

"Absolutely," said Phillip. "I love trees!"

"Me, too!" said all the children in unison.

"Yes, said Egg, "trees are wonderful to play in and are lovely to look at, but they also do an extremely important job for our planet, isn't that right, Your Majesty?"

"Thank you, Egg, yes, and we have been doing this job for many centuries. We trees help you humans to breathe. We oxygenate the air so that it is clean and safe. We take care of you," said the Tree King.

"Really? Oh, wow," said Reggie, "that's a really important job! And that means that Lewis Nero and the Rogue Beavers are hurting us as well!"

"Yes, Reggie, you are very clever to make that connection," said the Tree King looking pleased. "So, will you help us?"

"Absolutely! Count me in. What are we going to do?"

"Identify. Expose. Defuse." said Philip, in a precise, authoritative voice.

"Wow. said Reggie, deeply impressed, although he wasn't quite sure what he meant.

Philip noticed this and said, kindly,

"We have to identify these rotters, and we've already got a good idea who they are, but we also need to get evidence to prove they are destroying trees."

"Oh, I see! We need to catch them in the act, yes?"

"Exactly."

"And what does 'defuse' mean?"

"We have to make sure they can't do it again; we take away their power."

Stella spoke up – "Philip, we need a bit more detail, per favore."

"We'll call the police."

Alice turned to the whole group and said,

"So, there's no time to waste. We need to meet tonight at 9.00pm at this address," as she passed around a piece of paper to each of them. "This is where Lewis Nero and his gang hang out. Bring torches, cameras… I have a phone with a camera."

"But I normally go to bed at 8.00 o'clock!" said Reggie.

"Reggie, you'll have to sneak out. It's extremely important," said Alice, seriously.

Reggie looked back at Alice. She was no longer hiding behind her hair, instead, her head was up, and she looked ready to act. Reggie nodded in agreement.

CHAPTER FIVE

Later that evening, after his mum and dad kissed him goodnight, Reggie felt a twinge of regret that he was going to do something without telling his parents. However, then he thought about how much his dad loved trees and felt sure it was the right thing to do. He also made a promise to himself that he would tell his parents after the mission was over. So, he crept out of bed, got dressed, grabbed his rucksack, and packed it with a torch, a packet of crisps and a banana. Reggie had the idea that you always need snacks on a mission. He opened the window and his oak tree held out its branches ready to help him reach the ground. Then he dashed off to meet the others.

When Reggie reached the corner of his street, he found Philip waiting for him. Together they hurried along to the meeting point which was a few yards away from where Lewis Nero and his gang had their hide-out under an old, dis-used railway bridge.

"Okay, great, we're all here," said Philip in a low voice, "now we wait until they decide to move, and we follow them. Alice, Egg, and I have all got cameras."

Egg nodded his agreement.

…Reggie and Stella, when Egg gives the signal, switch your torches onto the gang so that we can take as clear a photo as possible. In the meantime, we must wait and keep completely silent," whispered Egg as they all edged closer. Soon they could hear Lewis Nero speaking.

"Now, you 'orrible lot!" said Lewis Nero in a gruff voice.

The beavers stared at him with disgust.

"Oh, forgive me, I don't know what comes over me sometimes. Dear Colleagues, our next assignment is at St Michael's in Priory Avenue."

"That's my school!" said Stella crossly, in a loud voice. "Oops. Mi scusi," she said, in a whisper.

"What an evil, horrible man he is," whispered Reggie.

"There are at least ten trees around the school site," continued Lewis Nero.

"We play in those trees!" whispered Stella.

"Don't worry, Stella, we are here to stop them." said Alice reassuringly.

"Boss, a word," said Taurus, the leader of the Rogue Beavers.

"Just before we get started, when exactly are we going to get paid?"

Yeah, yeah, we haven't had a bean," added Cougar, one of the other beavers.

"Ah, well, rest assured, you'll all get paid, handsomely. I just have a bit of a cash-flow problem, due to a temporary lack of liquidity... "

"How about putting that in plain English?" growled Taurus.

"He's flat broke. I'm off," said Cougar who turned to leave.

"Gentlemen, gentlemen! You misunderstand me. Tomorrow, I can pay you all tomorrow! We just need to complete tonight's task and all will be milk and honey!"

"Milk and honey, you having a larf? I want cash!"

"Yes, yes, I mean I can pay-you-all-your-money-tomorrow," said Lewis through gritted teeth and an unconvincing smile.

"Conference," said Taurus and the beavers huddled together at a distance from Lewis Nero.

"I don't trust him!" growled one beaver.
"I think he's stringing us along – he's got no money!"
"But he already owes us a load of dosh…"

Taurus turned back to Lewis.

"No more work after tonight – and you pay us first thing tomorrow!"

'Suits me,' thought Lewis to himself, 'I don't need them after tonight! Ha ha. I've got another bunch of mugs on board after this.'

"Agreed!" he said, "now can we get a move on?"

After some low muttering and grumbling, the beavers nodded their heads and set off for the school.

Okay, let's follow them, but keep quiet everyone," said Philip.

As they reached the school, the beavers split up and prepared to attack the tree trunks. Some of the trees had swings and they chewed through the ropes. Then Taurus sent a secret call to the other beavers which humans cannot hear.

"What is it?" said Cougar in reply.

"Kids. I can smell kids!"

Just then, Stella and Reggie switched on the torches and Philip, Egg and Alice got ready to take their photos, but it was too late! The beavers had burrowed into the ground and were nowhere to be seen. Lewis stood alone in the torchlight. He was furious. He turned to run away but caught his foot on one of the damaged ropes of a swing and fell over. Quick as a flash, Reggie tied his hands with the rope while Philip and Stella sat on him.

"I'm calling the police," shouted Alice.

When the police arrived, they struggled to understand the explanation from the children, in between the angry shouts from Lewis, who said he was entirely innocent and it's the children who should be arrested for attacking him.

"Officer, I insist you get these children off me and let me go!" shouted Lewis.

Officer Goodman took Alice and Egg to one side and spoke quietly.

"We know about Lewis Nero, but, without any evidence, we have to let him go. Do you have any pictures?"

"No," said Alice glumly. "We didn't get a chance to take any photos."

"But we do have this," said Egg, in his cool, calm manner. He pressed a button on his phone.

"Dear colleagues, our next assignment is St Mary's in Priory Avenue
There are at least ten trees around the school site…"

It was the whole conversation between Lewis and the beavers! Everyone looked at Egg in surprise.

"I thought it would be a good idea to record them. I always like to have a back-up plan."

"Well done, young man," said Officer Goodman, "come and see me when you're a grown-up, we always need clever people like you!"

And turning to Lewis Nero, he pulled him up by his arm and said

"I'd like to invite you to have a little chat at the station, Mr Nero."

The children clapped their hands and gave each other pats and hugs of congratulations.

Not too far away, Taurus and Cougar were watching.

"Hmm, Taurus, that didn't work out well. All that work and no pay!" growled Cougar.

"Yes, maybe someone is trying to tell us that we shouldn't do business with dodgy characters like Lewis Nero. Anyway, Cougar, I'm sick of destroying trees, I'd like to go back to building things, dams, and stuff, you know what I mean, like in the good old days, what do you think?" and they wandered off into the night.

Officer Goodman had called a car to pick up the children and take them home. Reggie was the last to be dropped off. The officers wanted to knock on the door, but Reggie persuaded them to let him go in by the garden.

"I'll be okay, I promise!" he said as he dashed across the lawn to where his oak tree had already lowered its branches to lift him up to his bedroom window.

"It went very well, Your Majesty," said Reggie to the Tree King.

"I know, Reggie, I saw it on the monitor. Well done, all of you did an excellent job. You have saved many trees today. Thank you."

Oh, well, you're welcome. I'm not sure I did that much, really."

"Oh, but you did. And never underestimate how important it is to be kind, Reggie. Problems cannot be solved if no one cares. Remember that.
Good night, Reggie."

"Good night, Your Majesty."

As Reggie began to change into his pyjamas, he gave a great big yawn.
He lay down on his bed, looking out at the stars as they peeped through the swaying branches of his mighty oak tree.

The background to the creation of the story of Reggie Ruby, the Pirate of the Trees

Mr Saurabh Jain, who is a Consultant Ophthalmologist (this is the correct spelling, Reggie!) knows an enormous amount about this eye condition and he has treated many children and adults.

Mr Jain is also Clinical Director at the Royal Free Hospital, London. He generously advised Lucia on the aspects of the story that related to squints in children and adults.

Lucia, who writes children's books, wanted to write an adventure story that includes children with a squint. Lucia also had strabismus (a squint), as an adult.

Mr Jain was very kind in helping Lucia with the story to ensure that she reflected the condition correctly in the book. Even better, Mr Jain fixed Lucia's strabismus!

Here is a message from Mr Jain, the inspiration for Mr June (did you guess?)

Hello!

I hope you enjoyed reading Reggie Ruby, the Pirate of the Trees. As you know, Reggie and Alice both have an eye condition called strabismus, and we also call the same condition a squint. It's very important that we all look after our eyes because they do a great job for us. So, here are some simple suggestions from me to help you to look after your eyes:

1. Don't spend too long on your tech devices, and when you are using them, take regular breaks, look away from the screen – or better still, go outside in the fresh air!

2. Wash your hands regularly – sometimes dirt gets in our eyes from our hands and can cause irritation.

3. Have a regular eye check – your parents will probably take care of that for you.

4. Eat carrots! Well, not just carrots. A good, healthy diet will help you have good general health and that will help you look after your eyes.

5. If you are worried about your eyes, tell an adult.

With warmest wishes from

Mr Jain

Saurabh Jain FRCOphth FHEA
Consultant Ophthalmologist and Clinical Director
Royal Free Hospital, London

Education Officer
British and Irish Paediatric Ophthalmology and Strabismus Association
Biposa.org.uk

www.saurabhjain.co.uk
Author of *Simplifying Strabismus: A Practical Approach to Diagnosis and Management*

Frans Wesselman, Artist

When Frans Wesselman is not drawing illustrations for Lucia, he works as a printmaker and stained-glass artist. He is a member of the Royal Society of Painter-Printmakers and the Contemporary Glass Society.

You can see more of his work at

www.fwstainedglass.co.uk

About the author:

Portrait by Anne Bowes*

Lucia Wilson is a British-born Anglo-Burmese writer of poetry, lyrics, and stories for all ages. She is a member of SACEM and PRS and lives in London. She collaborated on the albums, SHOW and The Devil in Me with French artist Victor de Sveynes and composer/musician, Maurice Tragni.

*annebowesillustration/Instagram

Other children's books by Lucia include:

The Adventures of Cedric the Bear which was created in collaboration with illustrator and jewellery designer, Anne Bowes and the original creator of Cedric, the physical bear, Katie Eggington,

www.cedricthebear.com

All illustrations by Frans Wesselman

Cover designed by Anne Bowes
Central illustration by Millie Wilson

Lucia is also the author of The Karloff Tiara, a fairy tale for grown-ups and tiara-wearers everywhere!

Cover illustration by Anne Bowes

You can find out more about Lucia's work at
www.luciawilson.co.uk and
www.cedricthebear.com

All publications are available on various online outlets including Amazon, Waterstones, Barnes and Noble.

Printed in Great Britain
by Amazon

84886741R00031